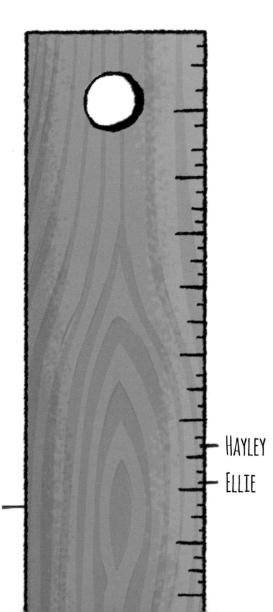

To my daughters,

Hayley and Ellie.

Your height does not equate to your worth. Don't let being small stop you from having big dreams.

HAYLEY

ELLIE

www.mascotbooks.com

being small

Second Printing. This Mascot Books edition printed in 2019.

For more information, please contact:
Mascot Books
620 Herndon Parkway #320
Herndon, VA 20170
info@mascotbooks.com

Library of Congress Control Number: 2018910678

CPSIA Code: PRT0519B
ISBN-13: 978-1-64307-127-5

Printed in the United States

being small

(Isn't So Bad After All)

Lori Orlinsky

illustrated by
Vanessa
Alexandre

My head is spinning,
and my throat is red.

I'm feeling crummy!
I'm staying in bed.

My eyes are itchy and
my ears really ache.

Going to school today
would be a mistake.

You're cool to the touch!
You don't look sick.

Could this be some kind of trick?

Because Mother knows
best, that's how I know.

Something's up, and you
don't *want* to go.

You're a wonderful child,
so smart and strong.

Come sit on my lap and
tell me what's wrong.

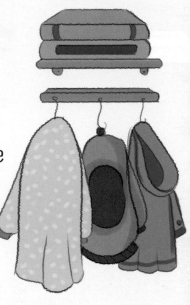

Well, the yardstick at school measures how much we've grown,

But with my name at the bottom, I feel so alone.

My friends can reach the cubbies, light switch, and sink,

While I stand on a stool when I want a drink.

FRIENDS

Helpers

Classroom Rules ♥

1.
2.
3.
4.
5.

AIDEN

AUDREY

My feet just dangle when I sit in a chair.
I can only go on rides with a high pony in my hair.

The shallow pool water comes up past my nose.

My feet always hurt from standing on my toes.

It seems like sports are made for kids who are tall.

I can't even get my hands on the ball.

They call me "Shorty," "Peanut," "Munchkin," and "Squirt."

Looking up all the time makes my neck really hurt!

I have to walk twice as fast as my friends.
My pants are like tunnels—the hole never ends.

When it's time to form teams, I'm always the last pick.

That's why today I'm pretending to be sick.

Don't you see that being small

Really is no fun at all?

Oh honey, try not to feel blue.

There's so much that small kids like you can do.

When playing limbo, you can get really low.
You give others a clear view when seeing a show.

Your posture is perfect because you don't slouch.
Your whole body can fit on our tiniest couch!

You're the last one to get wet when it rains,
And you have the most leg room when we fly on a plane.

Your feet never touch the end of the bed.
You can climb almost anywhere without bumping your head.

You can squeeze through a fence to fetch a lost ball,
And have a shorter drop if you happen to fall.

Mr. Doug's Pre-K Class

What about class photos? You're the first one they see!

You don't have to duck under any branches on a tree.

You can wiggle into the
cart at the grocery store,

And squish into the spaces
you want to explore.

I hope you don't feel upset by your height.

You can do anything when you give it your might.

You have so much to offer
because of your size.

Take it from me, your
mom who is wise.

You're totally right about the things you say.

I feel so much better when you put it that way.

I'm off to learn, play, and have fun, too!

I'll try out the things only *I* can do.

I went to school, and I'm happy to report,
As it turns out, I *like* being short!

I got to see, once and for all,
That being small isn't so bad after all.

the end

About the Author

Lori Orlinsky is a 5' 1" (on a good day, with heels and big hair) writer, member of the Society of Children's Book Writers and Illustrators, marketing director, and mom who lives in Chicago. She was inspired to tell this story after her own real-life experiences raising two little ladies. She wishes this story was around when she was growing up.

Acknowledgments

A special thank you to the people who matter the most in my life and have provided me with support and encouragement as I pursued my dream: My husband, Brian; Mom and Dad; my sister, Alyssa; and my best friend, Steph.

This book is dedicated to my Grandma Dina, a remarkable woman who showed me how to find inner strength in myself and the good in everyone. These are the messages I hope to convey to all children, big and small, with this book. Here's to you, Grandma. I know you and Grandpa are proudly reading this together in Heaven.